D0969470

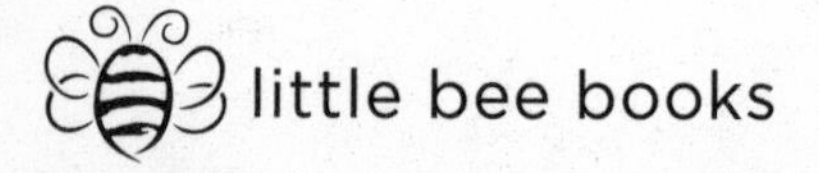

An imprint of Bonnier Publishing USA
251 Park Avenue South, New York, NY 10010

Manufactured in the United States of America LB 0417
ISBN: 978-1-4998-0398-3 (hc)
ISBN: 978-1-4998-0397-6 (pbk)
First Edition 10 9 8 7 6 5 4 3 2 1

Library of Congress Cataloging-in-Publication Data
is available upon request.

littlebeebooks.com
bonnierpublishingusa.com

Tales of SASHA

A New Friend

by Alexa Pearl
illustrated by Paco Sordo

little bee books

Contents

CHAPTER 1

Just Like Me

"Wait for me!" cried Sasha. She tried to catch up. She flew higher. She flapped her wings faster, but she still couldn't reach them.

Thick clouds rolled in, making it hard to see. Now she didn't know which way to turn. Then Sasha's breath caught in her throat.

Three horses flew out of a large cloud! One was yellow, one was blue, and one was purple. Their colorful wings shone bright against the gray sky. They were just like her. They were horses that could fly!

Sasha had never met another flying horse before. She just *had* to talk to them—now!

The three horses darted in and out of the clouds. They flew in crazy patterns.

"Wait for me!" she called again.

The three flying horses didn't wait.

Sasha was the fastest horse in her valley. She had won every running race. But flying was different than running. Horses didn't fly in a straight line.

"Keep going!" Wyatt called to her from the beach. The sand at his hooves sparkled with magical jewels. He raised his tail in a salute.

Sasha saluted back. Wyatt was her best friend. He had traveled all the way from their home in Verdant Valley to Crystal Cove with her.

"That must be Sapphire!" Wyatt pointed at the blue horse.

Sasha flapped her wings as fast as she could. She had heard stories about Sapphire, but she'd never met her. Sasha had never met *any* flying horses. Until now, she'd thought she was the only one. She had so many questions for them.

"Sapphire! I'm back!" cried Sasha.

Sapphire swooped low and out of sight.

She didn't hear me, thought Sasha.

Then Sasha spotted the yellow horse. She sped over to him.

"I just learned to fly!" she called.

The yellow horse soared higher and out of sight.

He doesn't care, thought Sasha.

The purple horse zoomed by.

"Hello!" called Sasha.

The purple horse didn't answer. Instead, she tucked her head and somersaulted in the air.

Sasha gasped. That was amazing!

“Your turn,” called the purple horse.

Sasha looked around. Who was she talking to?

The purple horse pointed her braided tail at Sasha.

“Me?” Sasha gulped. She didn’t know if she could do gymnastics and fly at the same time.

The purple horse waited.

Was this a test? If she passed, would the purple horse answer her questions? Sasha took a deep breath. *You can do this,* she told herself. *Head first, legs in, tuck, and roll. Go!*

The world spun upside down. Wind rushed up her nostrils, and her stomach twisted. Then she was upright again and flying. She heard Wyatt cheer. She had done it!

The purple horse smiled. “Fly with me!” she called.

Together, they soared through the clouds. The warm wind blew their manes. Sasha smiled. She had made her first friend in the Land of Flying Horses.

CHAPTER 2

A New Friend

The purple horse and Sasha glided down to the beach. Sasha's hooves kicked up a huge spray of sand and jewels as she skidded to a stop.

The purple horse laughed. "What's with your landing?"

"Sorry." Sasha bit her lip. "I just started flying."

The purple horse's violet eyes grew wide. "You *just* got your wings? So cool! I got mine last year."

Sasha admired the purple horse's shimmering wings. "Yours are so much fluffier than mine. Why?"

"I put honey on them to make them fluffy," said the purple horse.

"Really?" Sasha wrinkled her nose. That sounded gross.

"*Not* really." The purple horse laughed again. "Honey would make my feathers stick together. I made that up. There's no big secret. Your wings will grow fluffier the more you use them."

"Does that make flying easier?" asked Sasha.

"So much easier! Fluffy wings are powerful." She fanned out her wings and struck a pose. "Don't I look superpowerful?"

The purple horse laughed again. Sasha found herself laughing, too.

"I'm Kimani." The purple horse stood nose-to-nose with Sasha. "I've never seen you here in Crystal Cove."

"I'm not from here," said Sasha. "I live in Verdant Valley."

"Where's that?" asked Kimani.

"It's down the beach, over the lake, through the fields, and on the other side of the big trees," said Sasha.

"You live on the *other side* of the big trees? For real?" cried Kimani.

Sasha nodded. "I was left there when I was a baby. There was a note on my golden blanket. I don't know who left me or why. I came here to find out. My name is Sasha."

Kimani reared up on her hind legs. "*You're* Sasha?"

"You've heard of me?" Sasha's heart thumped with excitement.

Kimani looked a little nervous. "You're the *real* Sasha?"

"I guess." Sasha wasn't sure what that meant.

Kimani scanned the sky as if she were looking for someone. Then she twirled her tail. Three twirls one way, and then three twirls the other way.

Sasha had never seen a tail move like that. “Is everything okay?” she asked.

Kimani quickly stopped spinning her tail. “Of course! I just, um, think the sky looks really pretty today,” she replied nervously.

“Okay . . . ,” Sasha said, but she wasn’t convinced.

“Hey!” Kimani exclaimed. “Who’s that?”

CHAPTER 3

The Toucan Brings a Message

"Ouch! These red gems get hot in the sun!" Wyatt galloped toward them.

"That's my friend, Wyatt," Sasha told Kimani.

Kimani stared at him. "Didn't you get your wings yet?"

"I'm never getting wings. Horses don't have wings," said Wyatt.

"Are you sure?" Kimani spread her wings wide.

"Horses don't have wings where we come from," explained Sasha. "I was the only one."

"That sounds like a terrible place," said Kimani.

"Not at all," said Sasha. "Verdant Valley is great. We have a school and big fields to run in."

"We have a stream with cold water and a tall mountain with wildflowers," added Wyatt.

"My family is there." Sasha told Kimani about her mother, her father, and her older sisters Zara and Poppy.

"None of them have wings," Kimani pointed out. "You should stay here. Crystal Cove is the Land of Flying Horses."

"Stay here?" Now Wyatt reared back.

"Don't worry," Sasha told Wyatt. They'd left home at sunrise, and now it was sunset. Sasha missed her family. "I'm not staying. I only came to find other winged horses."

"It's getting dark." Wyatt tugged Sasha. They had a long journey back home.

"Don't leave!" Kimani looked at the sky again. "You have to wait."

At that moment, a toucan swooped down and landed on Kimani's back. "I got your signal," said the toucan.

So that's what the tail twirling was about, thought Sasha.

"I have a message from Sapphire. She wants to see the new horse now." The toucan spoke in a booming voice.

Sasha turned to Wyatt. Many years ago, Sapphire had met their old teacher, Caleb. They were both foals, and Caleb had helped her when she'd hurt her wing. Before she flew away, she'd given him a magical map. Sasha and Wyatt had used that map today to find the flying horses. Wyatt knew how important meeting Sapphire was to Sasha.

Wyatt nodded. "Okay. Let's go."

"Not you," said the toucan. "Just Sasha."

"Wyatt is not one of us," explained Kimani. "He doesn't have wings."

Sasha's ears flattened against her head. The horses at home used to say she was different because she daydreamed about faraway places. Sometimes they wouldn't be her partner at school.

"I won't go without him." Sasha's voice sounded strong, but her knees felt wobbly.

Kimani shared a secret look with the toucan. Sasha was worried. Had she ruined her big chance to talk to Sapphire?

Kimani shrugged. “Okay. Wyatt can come along.”

Sasha and Wyatt grinned.

The toucan led the way. The three horses headed down the beach and entered a jungle. Thick tropical plants crowded close together. Fuzzy caterpillars chewed fan-shaped leaves. Blue dragonflies swarmed above their heads. The air grew warm and sticky.

Sasha blew her forelock out of her eyes. She wished for the cool shade of the cottonwood tree back home.

Wyatt tried to munch a big flower.

"I wouldn't eat that," warned Kimani.

"Whoa!" Wyatt jumped back as a red horse poked her nose out from behind the flower.

Sasha was about to tease Wyatt for being a scaredy-cat. Then she saw them.

All of them.

CHAPTER 4 Who Are You, Really?

Sasha turned slowly in a circle.

Pink. Lavender. Turquoise. Horses of all colors hid in the leafy plants. They stared at Sasha and whispered. Were they talking about her?

"What's going on?" whispered Sasha.

"They're friendly." Kimani pushed her forward. "They came to greet you."

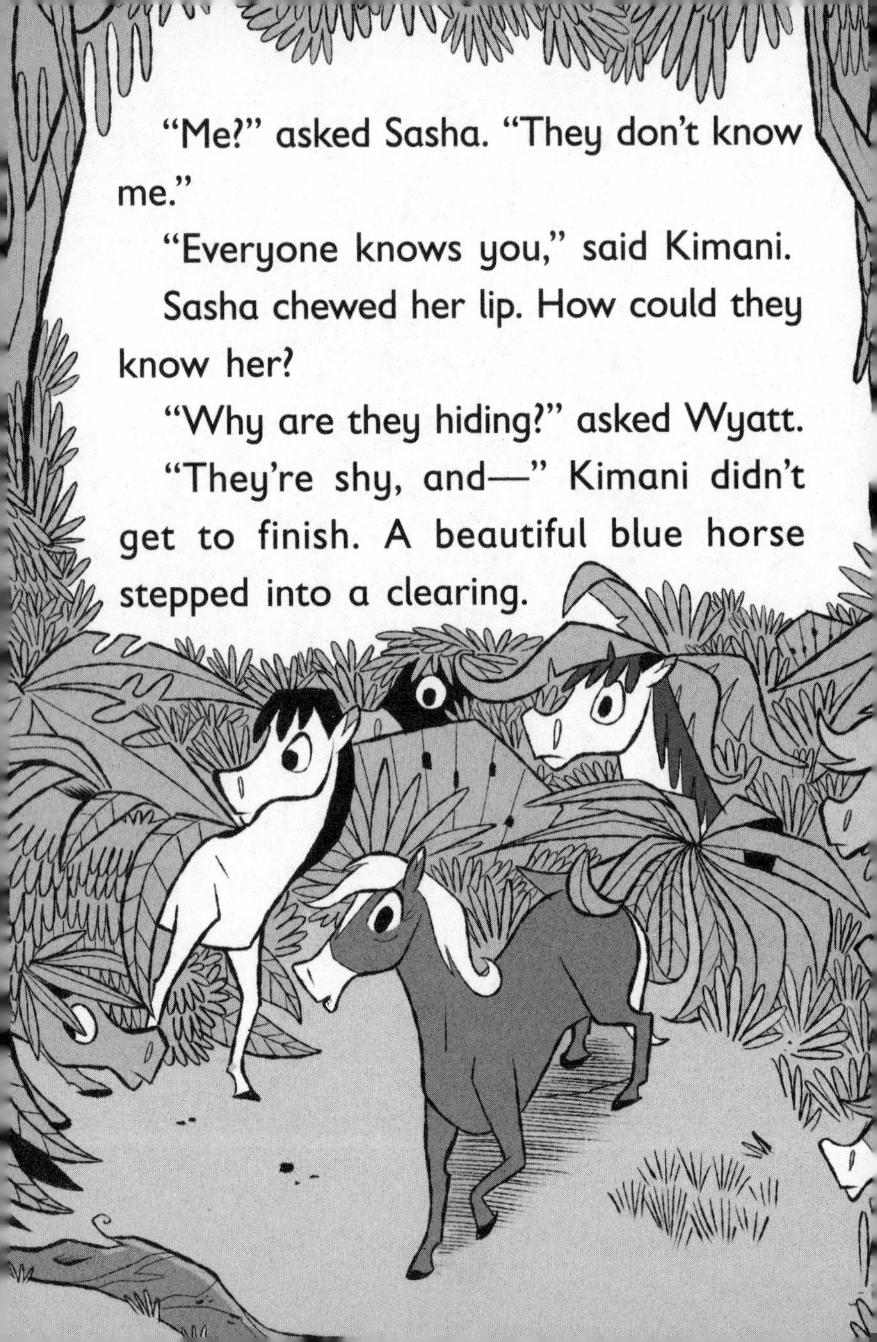

“Me?” asked Sasha. “They don’t know me.”

“Everyone knows you,” said Kimani.

Sasha chewed her lip. How could they know her?

“Why are they hiding?” asked Wyatt.

“They’re shy, and—” Kimani didn’t get to finish. A beautiful blue horse stepped into a clearing.

"Sapphire!" Sasha began to trot toward her.

"Whoa!" A yellow horse jumped out and blocked her path. "I need to check you first."

"Check me for what?" asked Sasha.

"I need to be sure you are who you say you are," he said.

"Who else would I be?" Sasha was confused.

"We should go," whispered Wyatt.

Sasha knew if she was going to get any answers, they would come from Sapphire. She locked eyes with the yellow horse. He was larger than any horse Sasha had ever met. "Fine. Check me."

He walked around Sasha. "She has a white patch on her back. It is the shape of a cloud."

A horse in the plants let out a gasp.

"I've always had that patch," said Sasha. "That's where my wings come out from."

The yellow horse looked inside her mouth. "She is missing a back tooth on the left side," he said.

"It's been missing since I was born," said Sasha.

Another horse gasped.

The yellow horse nodded at the ground behind her. "Are these your hoof prints?"

"Yes." Sasha saw for the first time that her hoof print was different from Wyatt and Kimani's. Hers had a heart shape in the middle.

"The patch, the tooth, and the hoof print all prove it," said the yellow horse. "She really is Sasha. Sasha has returned!"

The colorful herd of horses burst out of their hiding spots. With a *whoosh*, they opened their wings and let out a huge cheer.

They were cheering for her!

CHAPTER

5 Let's Dance

Sapphire walked toward her. "How did you find your way back to us?"

Sasha showed her the blue feather and the magical map. "You left these with Caleb."

"He saved my life." Sapphire closed her eyes, remembering him. "If he hadn't fixed my wing, I would've been in danger."

"Danger? Why?" asked Sasha.

Sapphire let out a long breath. "That's a story for another time."

Now that Sapphire was here, Sasha was nervous. Sasha decided to ask her most important question first. “The note on my blanket said: ‘Please keep Sasha safe until we can see her again.’ Did you write that note? Did you leave me in Verdant Valley?”

“It wasn’t me,” said Sapphire.

Sasha’s stomach dropped. She’d been so sure it had been Sapphire.

“I did pick Verdant Valley. Caleb showed me that the horses there were kind,” said Sapphire.

Sasha thought about this. "If you chose the place, does that mean you know where I came from?"

Before Sapphire could answer, music filled the air. A pink horse began to sing. Others tapped their hooves in time with the beat.

"Enjoy the party!" cried Sapphire. "It's for you. We'll talk tomorrow." She hurried away.

Fireflies filled the night sky. They spelled SASHA with their lights. A huge apple-and-carrot cake was wheeled in front of her.

“Don’t you think it’s strange that you’re such a big deal here?” asked Wyatt.

“Maybe, but I like it.” Sasha had never had a big party before. She tapped her hooves happily to the music.

“Let’s dance!” Kimani lifted her body several inches off the ground.

“How do I do that?” Sasha wanted to hover like a hummingbird, too.

"It's easy." Kimani showed Sasha how to move her wings in small circles. Sasha rose off the ground.

"Time to twirl!" called Kimani. Together, they twirled above Wyatt.

"You should dance, too," called Sasha.

"I'm stuck down here," said Wyatt.

"You can dance there." Sasha wished Wyatt wasn't being such a party pooper.

Kimani and Sasha twirled until they were both dizzy.

Thwack! Wyatt's tail playfully swatted Sasha. She dropped to the ground.

"You can't do that." Kimani narrowed her eyes at Wyatt.

"I do it all the time." Wyatt was forever swatting his tail at Sasha.

"You don't get it," said Kimani. "She's *Sasha*."

"I know who she is." Wyatt turned to Sasha. "It's time to go home."

"We're having peppermint ice cream soon," said Kimani.

"That sounds yummy." Then Sasha saw Wyatt scowl. "But we need to go back."

"It's too late to leave. The ferry doesn't run after dark. Wyatt can't get across the lake," said Kimani. The lake was too wide to swim across, and Wyatt couldn't fly.

"Stay here tonight. We'll have a sleepover!" Kimani's violet eyes twinkled with excitement.

"Great idea," said Sasha.

Wyatt frowned. He didn't think so. "What about Caleb? He's waiting for us."

"No problem." Kimani waved over a firefly. She whispered in his ear, and then he flew away. "He'll bring Caleb a message right away."

Sasha and Kimani danced and danced. Wyatt stood silently near a group of other horses not dancing.

When Sasha finally took a break, Wyatt pulled her aside. “I need to talk to you.”

“The ice cream is melting,” called Kimani.

“Wait until later,” Sasha told Wyatt. She hurried to get ice cream.

Afterward, Kimani took them to her room. All the horses lived in caves carved into the cliffs. Soft patterned blankets covered the floors and the walls. Fluffy fur pillows were scattered everywhere. Sasha loved how cozy it was.

“We can sleep over here.” Wyatt pushed together two pillows.

Sasha yawned. She was tired from their long day.

“Don’t sleep yet,” said Kimani. “Have you ever flown in the moonlight?”

Sasha's white patch itched with excitement. It did that when her body wanted to fly. "Could I touch a star?" she asked Kimani.

"Let's try." Kimani grinned.

"What about me?" Wyatt frowned. "I wanted to talk to you, Sasha."

Sasha hated not including Wyatt, but Kimani was her first flying horse friend. Tomorrow, she would go home. No one there would fly with her through the stars. She'd have plenty of time to talk to Wyatt later.

"I'll be right back," Sasha promised him.

The world below was dark and silent as the two horses flew through the night sky. Sasha tried to touch a star. She couldn't reach it. Stars were much farther away than they looked!

Sasha waved to a snowy-white owl that glided by. She wondered if Wyatt were looking up. Did he see her tail sparking with magic in the darkness?

Together, Sasha and Kimani somersaulted in the moonlight.

CHAPTER 6 Gone!

Wyatt was fast asleep when they got back. Sasha didn't wake him. She went to sleep, too.

At dawn, Wyatt woke up.

"Sasha," whispered Wyatt. His breath was warm against her ear. "Sasha."

She didn't answer. She was still sleeping.

Wyatt nudged her. "It's time to go home."

Sasha opened one eye. Pale morning sunlight poked through the cave door. How could that be? She felt as if she'd just gone to bed. "Not yet," she mumbled.

Wyatt kept on nudging her.

"Go away," she grumbled. She was so tired. She closed her eyes again.

Hours later, Sasha finally woke up. Bright sunshine filled the cave.

"Hey, there." Kimani stood by the open door. "There's leftover cake. Want some?"

"Sure." Sasha stretched her legs. "Where's Wyatt?"

"He went home," said Kimani.

"He went without me?" Sasha couldn't believe it.

Kimani shrugged. "He was up early. He tried to wake you."

Sasha winced. She remembered now.

"I told him not to bother you. Besides, we don't need him. He's better off in Verdant Valley," said Kimani.

"You *told* him to go?" Sasha's voice rose.

"He wanted to go," said Kimani. "He was upset."

Sasha felt horrible. She had been so caught up with her new friend that she hadn't realized he was upset.

"I've got good news!" cried Kimani. "Sapphire has been waiting for you to wake up."

"I need to find Wyatt," said Sasha.

"He'll be fine." Kimani pointed over at the golden door where Sapphire lived. "Don't you want answers to your questions? This is your chance."

Sasha let Kimani push her toward Sapphire's home.

"Greetings!" The toucan opened the door. "Sapphire's almost ready. Please enjoy this breakfast."

He placed an enormous platter in front of Sasha. Sunflowers, marigolds, and daisies were piled high. There was one bowl filled with honey and one bowl filled with raspberry jam.

Sasha licked her lips. She leaned forward to dip a daisy into the honey.

The sweet smell made her think of Wyatt. Wyatt loved wildflowers. She remembered the day they climbed Mystic Mountain to search for the tastiest flowers and her wings had popped out for the very first time. Wyatt had been so happy for her. He had wanted her to find the flying horses. He had gone with her through the scary forest when Caleb couldn't make it. He'd been by her side the whole time. Now he was by himself. What if he didn't know how to get home? He didn't have the magic map.

Sasha spit out the flower. She couldn't stay here any longer.

"Kimani," said Sasha, "tell Sapphire I have to go."

"You can't!" cried Kimani.

"I need to make sure Wyatt is okay." Wyatt was her oldest friend. She'd been wrong to ignore him. She wasn't going to leave him alone now.

"Go with her," the toucan told Kimani.

"You don't have to." Sasha knew Kimani didn't like Wyatt all that much.

"I want to help," said Kimani. "I know this land better than you."

CHAPTER 7 Bend, Cross, Spring!

Sasha and Kimani trotted down the beach.

"Hello!" A peacock stepped out and opened his tail feathers.

"We're looking for my friend." Sasha had met this peacock yesterday.

"Eyes in the sky see so much more," said the peacock.

"We can't fly," explained Kimani. "We're searching for hoof prints. Her friend doesn't fly."

"He's heading to the big trees," said Sasha.

The peacock's feathers quivered. "You're going into the big trees, too?"

Kimani nodded.

The peacock lowered his voice. "Keep eyes open for the little ones."

Sasha wanted to ask who the little ones were, but a troop of spider monkeys rode by on scooters. Kimani stopped one to ask about Wyatt.

"He was meeting the morning ferry," said the spider monkey.

Sasha and Kimani set off at a gallop. They reached the edge of the big lake.

"Is that him on the ferry?" asked Kimani.

Sasha squinted at the far side of the lake. Wyatt stood on a raft that was paddled by three beavers. They watched him step onto the far dock and trot away.

Sasha pawed the ground. What should she do? It would take a long time for the beavers to paddle back to pick them up.

"Let's fly," said Kimani.

Sasha stared at the water in front of her. "I can't. I need a running start to take off."

"No, you don't. Bend your knees low." Kimani showed her how. "Then cross your eyes."

"What?" That sounded so silly.

"Do you want to catch up to Wyatt?" asked Kimani.

Sasha nodded. The longer she waited, the farther away he was getting.

"Bend your knees, cross your eyes, then spring up fast," said Kimani.

Sasha bent, crossed, and sprang. She was flying! She couldn't believe how many new things Kimani had taught her in the past day.

She and Kimani flew over the lake in minutes. Wyatt had already trotted through the field of neon flowers. Now he stepped into the woods beyond the big trees.

Sasha landed and ran with a burst of speed towards Wyatt.

"Stop!" Kimani cut in front of her.

Sasha pulled back so she wouldn't crash into Kimani. "What's wrong?"

"You can't go into the woods," said Kimani. "There is danger there for flying horses."

Sasha remembered that Kimani had made up that story about honey turning wings fluffier. "You're making this up because you don't want Wyatt around."

"I'm not making it up," said Kimani. "You're my friend, and I want you to be safe. You have wings now, and others know it. There's danger for us."

What should I do? Sasha wondered. *Should I trust Kimani? Or should I follow Wyatt?*

CHAPTER

8 A Big Sneeze

Sasha dodged around Kimani. She sped toward the trees. She was fine yesterday in the woods. She was going after Wyatt.

Sasha tried to remember the path home through the woods. The trees were close together and tangled with one another.

She looked behind her. No Kimani. She was by herself. She followed the map until she spotted green fields beyond the trees—and Wyatt! He was leaving the woods.

"Wy—" She started to call for him. Then she felt pricks along her back. What was that? It felt like tiny feet were running on her back. How could that be? What was on her? She twisted to see.

Oh! Five tiny creatures stood on her back. Everything about them was pointy. Pointy nose. Pointy chin. Pointy ears. Pointy elbows and fingers. They had bright green skin and wore outfits made from leaves.

She tried to shake them off. They stayed on.

"Help!" She felt something tug at one of her wings.

Wyatt hurried back into the woods at the sound of her cries. He swatted them with his tail, but their tiny feet seemed glued to her back. Two more dropped onto her from the tree above.

"What should we do?" Sasha was scared.

"I don't know." Wyatt looked scared, too.

"Sneeze," called someone from deep in the woods.

Sasha spotted Kimani hiding behind a nearby tree.

"Come out and help," called Wyatt.

"I can't," said Kimani. "They'll get me, too. Wyatt, you need to sneeze on them."

Wyatt didn't move.

"Do it fast!" called Kimani.

This is the danger Kimani warned about, Sasha realized. *She had been telling the truth.*

"Trust her," Sasha told Wyatt.

Wyatt tried to sneeze. Only a cough came out. He tried again. The little creatures started tugging on Sasha's wings.

"I can't sneeze on command," he said.

Kimani raced from the safety of her hiding spot. She picked a dandelion from the ground. She waved it under Wyatt's nose.

A-a-choo! Wyatt let out an enormous sneeze near Sasha's back. Snot covered the little creatures and unglued their feet. They fell to the ground.

For a moment, Sasha stared at them. They were so tiny! Then they grabbed onto her tail. They began to climb it, using the hair as a rope.

Sasha's surprise turned to anger. Hot white sparks shot out of her tail, shocking the creatures. They scurried into the bushes and wrapped themselves in leaves until they couldn't be seen.

"We need to get out of here," said Kimani.

They all quickly hurried into Verdant Valley.

CHAPTER 9

Two Friends

Sasha was so happy to see the green fields of home again.

"I didn't listen and left you out. I'm sorry," Sasha told Wyatt. "Is that why you left?"

Wyatt kicked at the grass. "You didn't need me. You found a new friend. I thought you wanted to stay with her."

"I'm your friend, too," said Sasha. "I *do* need you, don't you see? You just saved me."

"It wasn't only me. Kimani helped, too." Wyatt gave Kimani a shy smile. "We worked together."

Kimani smiled back. "That was a good sneeze. You've got a lot of sticky snot."

"No wings, but plenty of snot. That's me." Wyatt laughed.

"We all have something that makes us special," teased Sasha. She was lucky she'd had two good friends to help her.

“So what were those things?” Wyatt asked Kimani.

"They're plant pixies, the enemy of flying horses. They want to steal our power of flight," said Kimani.

"How?" asked Wyatt.

"They need to pluck two wing feathers—one from the right wing and one from the left wing. The feathers fit into a harness that they wear. With both feathers in the harness, the plant pixie can fly," explained Kimani.

"I have plenty of feathers," said Sasha. "I could share some."

Kimani shook her head. "It doesn't work that way. Every time a feather is taken from a flying horse, she grows weaker. Soon, she can't fly or even gallop."

Sasha didn't like the sound of that.

"Plant pixies live in the woods," said Kimani. "A spell was placed on Verdant Valley so they can't come here. It was very important that you grew up safe."

Sasha titled her head. "I don't understand. Why did I need to be kept safe?"

"That's what I've been trying to tell you," said Wyatt. "I heard the yellow horse talking about you at the party."

"You know?" asked Kimani.

"I do," said Wyatt. "Should I tell her?"

"Tell me what?" Sasha stared at her two friends.

Wyatt and Kimani spoke at the same time. "You are the Lost Princess."

Read on for a sneak peek from the fourth book in the Tales of Sasha series!

#4

Tales of SASHA

Princess Lessons

by Alexa Pearl

illustrated by Paco Sordo

CHAPTER 1 Little Fairy Creatures

"Did you hear that?" Sasha lifted her ears.

"Hear what?" asked her better-than-best friend, Wyatt.

"A crunch from under this boysenberry bush." Sasha stepped forward to look. "Is it them?"

"Stay back!" cried Wyatt. "I'll look."

Sasha frowned. She should look first—not Wyatt. She was the brave one. Everyone knew that.

But everything had changed this week.

She wasn't a regular horse like Wyatt anymore. She was a flying horse—and flying horses were in danger.

"Sasha! You're home!" Poppy squealed and trotted toward her sister.

There were three sisters in Sasha's family. Sasha was the youngest, Zara was the oldest, and Poppy was in the middle. Poppy was the fancy sister. She wore flowers in her mane and tail.

Sasha nuzzled Poppy. She was happy to be home in Verdant Valley. So much had happened this week. First, Sasha had discovered that she had wings and could fly. Then, she'd gone away to search for other flying horses.

"What's he doing?" cried Poppy. Wyatt's head was buried in the bushes. Leaves and berries dropped to the ground.

"Searching for plant pixies," said Sasha.

"For what?" Poppy usually knew everything, but she had never heard of plant pixies.

"Plant pixies are little fairy creatures who live in plants," said Sasha.

"How cute!" exclaimed Poppy.

"Not so much." Wyatt lifted his head. "These pixies may be tiny, but they can hurt a flying horse."

"Can I see a plant pixie?" asked Poppy.

"They're not here. He made the noise," Wyatt said, pointing to a chipmunk. The chipmunk shrugged, then grabbed a berry.

"Happy days!" A purple horse cantered out of the shadows. The tiny braids in her tail twirled as she ran.

Poppy's brown eyes grew wide. She had never seen a purple horse! Her coat was chestnut-brown and so was Wyatt's. Sasha was pale gray with a white patch on her back. All the horses in Verdant Valley were brown, white, black, or gray.

"Who are you?" Poppy asked.

"Kimani is my new friend. She lives in

Crystal Cove with the other flying horses. She flies, too," said Sasha.

Kimani opened her wings. Her feathers were deep violet.

Poppy wasn't sure what was more amazing—that her little sister had found other horses with wings or that the flying horses were so beautiful.

Kimani inspected Poppy's mane and tail. "Wow! I never knew regular horses were so glamorous. Can you put pretty flowers in my mane, too?"

"Sure!" Poppy smiled. Sasha wouldn't stand still when Poppy tried to decorate her mane. She turned to Sasha. "I like your new friend."

"Here comes your mom and Caleb." Wyatt pointed across the meadow.

Caleb, their teacher, was old and moved very slowly. Sasha knew it would be a while before they both reached her. She listened to Poppy and Kimani talk about using honeysuckle petals to make their manes smell nice.

"Boring!" Sasha spotted an apple on the ground. "Think fast!" she called to Wyatt.

She kicked the apple with her hoof. It sailed through the air toward him. Wyatt headed the apple back to her. She blocked it with one of her hind legs and knocked it back at him.

Then Wyatt kicked it too hard. The apple rolled under a large white mushroom nearby. Sasha bent to look for it.

A tiny, pointy face peered out at her from under the mushroom.

A plant pixie!